T0114913

Two Stories, ONE Hope!

Love's Persistent Call
& New WOLF

2nd Edition

Danny A. Hurd

WESTBOW
P R E S S®
A DIVISION OF THOMAS NELSON
& ZONDERVAN

WestBow Press books may be ordered through booksellers or by contacting:

WestBow Press
A Division of Thomas Nelson & Zondervan
1663 Liberty Drive
Bloomington, IN 47403
www.westbowpress.com
844-714-3454

All Scripture quotations are from the ESV® Bible (The Holy Bible, English
Standard Version®), copyright © 2001 by Crossway, a publishing ministry
of Good News Publishers. Used by permission. All rights reserved.

ISBN: 979-8-3850-1423-1 (sc)
ISBN: 979-8-3850-1424-8 (e)

Library of Congress Control Number: 2023923416

Print information available on the last page.

WestBow Press rev. date: 12/28/2023

DEDICATION

To God the Father, God the Son (Jesus), God the Holy Spirit, Jan, Loving Family, and Friends.

ABOUT THE BOOK

These are 2nd edition works of fiction. Most of the main ideas for both stories came before the latest world events, personal experiences/ worldview, and imagination. If you like it, share with others. If there are errors, I apologize, and will make corrections by hand in printed books and soft copies before further printings. Your understanding is appreciated. This is a ministry that I hope you will participate in by sharing this book, and more importantly, your own testimony and The Bible, with others. Jesus shared stories; let's do the same and encourage others!

PRAYER FOR READERS

Father, Dear Lord God, Thank You for Your mercy, blessings, and for opening eyes and hearts. Please help us love You and our neighbors and give us saving faith. All praise, glory, and thanks to You! In Jesus' Name. Amen. Love, Dan

CONTENTS

LOVE'S PERSISTENT CALL

CHAPTER 1

INTRODUCTION

God's Unusual Call

Have you ever been on the playground getting ready to play a game or sport that were made up of teams? If so, you may have noticed that what typically happened is the bigger, stronger, better players were selected first. Then smaller, less experienced, followed by many of us who never played before, but wanted to be included. Because of the shame associated with the process, this might have been especially heartbreaking for many. How does God call us? In 1 Cor. 1:26-29 we read,

> For consider your calling, brothers: not many of you were wise according to worldly standards, not many were powerful, not many were of noble birth. But God chose what is foolish in the world to shame the wise; God chose the weak in the world to shame the strong; God chose what was low and despised in the world, even things that are not, to bring to nothing things that are, so that

1

no human being might boast in the presence of God. (English Standard Version (ESV))

On the playground, as in life, humanity tends to pick the best, because we want to win, be popular, get bragging rights, or be number one. God does the opposite, because He calls the weak, despised, foolish, and that makes His call unusual in the traditional sense of our modern world. It proves He is who He says He is, and His will be done.

Irrevocable and Persistent Call

"For the gifts and calling of God are irrevocable" (Rom. 11:29 ESV).

What makes this "irrevocable" statement unique? From a worldly perspective, we might think that NOTHING is irrevocable. If somebody does anything wrong, violates a law, breaks a promise, or double-crosses us, they lose the privilege of any guarantee. How often do people hold grudges because they simply cannot let things go? "Who do they think they are dealing with? Don't they know who I am? My rights have been violated! There is nothing more important than me!" But not so with the Lord God. Later in the book, we will see a name in Revelation, "Faithful and True." If God says it, He does it. In Deut. 31:8, Moses spoke to Joshua,

"It is the Lord who goes before you. He will be with you; He will not leave you or forsake you. Do not fear or be dismayed" (ESV).

It is important that we see God bringing Joshua and Israel to it, and then eventually, through it (M. Pitts, Sermon, April 24, 2016).

The Story Ahead

Some of us have either assumed we lost our salvation or believed we were never saved. Let us face it; we lost hope! The bible's position is once saved, we are eternally secure. Why? Because God is Faithful and True. It is my hope you find the story interesting and valuable. How did the story develop? We are bombarded daily with information, so it is difficult not to form opinions. Hardly a day goes by when I do not ask, "What is going on?" Nothing shocks me anymore. Why? Consider national or institutionalized idolatry. Sound odd? Be prepared because the formula for the story includes current events, firsthand experiences, imagination, bible verses (with application), opinion, and lots of prayer. Hopefully, we can learn a lesson or two as we read and think through the process, always thanking God for His persistent, loving, and yes, unusual call.

CHAPTER 2

LITTLE GIRL WITH A BRIGHT FUTURE

Janesth

It was a beautiful day in late 1956, the day that Janice-Esther (Janesth) was born in southern California. She was the middle child of three. Her mother would often speak of Jesus as the savior, who came down from heaven, died on the cross for the faithful, and then God the Father proved His power by raising him again from the dead. When she was nine years old, Janesth asked Jesus to come into her heart and save her. Her mother said that God called her to be His adopted child. In fact, she often cited the following verses from Rom. 8:28-30, which Janesth did not fully understand at the time, but knew she could trust her mother. These verses became especially important to Janesth,

> And we know that for those who love God all
> things work together for good, for those who are
> called according to his purpose. For those whom

he foreknew he also predestined to be conformed
to the image of his Son, in order that he might be
the firstborn among many brothers. And those
whom he predestined he also called, and those
whom he called he also justified, and those whom
he justified he also glorified. (ESV)

Grown Up and Looking Back

When Janesth was growing up in the late fifties and early sixties,
life was very different. As she aged and got closer to retirement,
her thoughts reflected to her childhood. Everything seemed to
move so quickly today, and one of the reasons, she concluded, was
the rise in technology and innovation. Workers had substantial
amounts of information, data, and knowledge at their fingertips.
In many ways this made it easier to do work, but privacy issues
always created real concerns. Janesth was unusual in her work
performance because she never received reprimands. In fact, she
was frequently commended for outstanding performance. Most
of her co-workers did not have a similar work ethic, so poor
performance caused many administrative problems.

Since it was considered a failure to encourage assimilation for
supervisors if employees performed poorly, it became widespread
practice to overlook performance metrics, good or bad. Because
of these issues, and high supervisory termination levels, Janesth
never received future awards. It was considered unfair to give
awards to some employees and not others. These new management
techniques reduced their need to counsel deficient performance,
and good employees never "rocked the boat." Surprisingly,
management did not notice the unfairness of their employee
evaluations. At each year's end, they spent much time creating
surveys to determine why employee performance and attitudes
got lower.

God Brings Two People Together

In the eighties, Janesth was hiking with her Christian singles group, and met a man named Danall. He described himself as a "Christian with flaws." Janesth, intrigued by this, discovered he simply acknowledged his inability to do the right thing without God's help. Janesth had the same problem, and as they got to know each other, he asked her to marry him. They loved and supported each other in work, home, family, medical, and spiritual issues. They even led the youth group together for a short time. One especially meaningful memory was the way Danall had the youth put their prayer requests on yellow stickies. Each week they would look at the requests, and write an "A" on those that were answered. After a while, the board was covered with "As." God had blessed their prayers, service, and ministries. Each week they discussed joys, cares, and concerns, always ending in the Lord's prayer.

Danall

While growing up in Detroit, he recalled shootings, murders, and muggings. One poignant memory was often running from people chasing him. He frequently thought similar events might reoccur, so this exaggerated fear made him question his faith. In 1 Jn. 4:18 he read,

> "There is no fear in love, but perfect love casts out fear. For fear has to do with punishment, and whoever fears has not been perfected in love" (ESV).

He memorized the following verses and often repeated them to Janesth, who said, "Yes, I heard it before, but I know you are going to tell me anyway, so go ahead!" Then she smiled. Danall's favorite quotation came from Phil. 2:5-11,

> Have this mind among yourselves, which is yours in Christ Jesus, who, though he was in the form of God, did not count equality with God a thing to be grasped, but made himself nothing, taking the form of a servant, being born in the likeness of men. And being found in human form, he humbled himself by becoming obedient to the point of death, even death on a cross. Therefore God has highly exalted him and bestowed on him the name that is above every name, so that at the name of Jesus every knee should bow, in heaven and on earth and under the earth, and every tongue confess that Jesus Christ is Lord, to the glory of God the Father. (ESV)

Tragedy Strikes the Family

One day while doing some yard work, and out of nowhere, some men started harassing Danall. Using profanity and yelling, they hit him with sticks and rocks. In his usual nervous manner and thinking how this reminded him of growing up in Detroit, he just wanted to run away. As he fearfully stood there, he thought of Phil. 2:5-11 and spoke it word for word to the three men. They looked surprised that anybody would say that. Danall repeated the exact same words again. The men looked at each other, two pulled out guns, and shot Danall multiple times. He died instantly. One was caught and sent to prison. After completing 18 months, he was released. Janesth learned years later that he became a prison minister focusing on personal responsibility and accountability, frequently witnessing to others. As time went on and she learned more about God and His trustworthiness, she rejoiced that He was merciful, even after personal sins and tragedies.

Alone Again

Janesth was never the same from that day forward. She was fearful, and no matter how many times she tried to remember that perfect love casts out fear, she could not let it go. As she continued working, she noticed she had many health issues related to stress, nerves, heart, and panic. "Oh God, why did this happen?" Janesth remembered that she and Danall had written letters for each other in the event of the other's unexpected demise. In his letter she read,

> Oh precious, beautiful, and loved Janesth, If you are reading this, it means that God has taken me home. Please do not be troubled too long because God knows best. You are the love of my life, and I pray God's greatest blessings and comfort for you. It is obvious that God has some additional work for you to do. Try not to let fear, anger, or sadness reign for long. God will comfort you, so please call on Him. When you can, please rejoice that I am home now, and look forward to our meeting again in heaven. Love Forever and Always, Danall

Sadness overwhelmed Janesth as she thought, "What else could there be for me to do? I am lonely, and need him to give me a push or guidance. Oh Lord, I am lost! Help me!" This happened daily and she was unable to get out of bed or sleep. Either way, exhaustion affected her work performance and she got little done.

Changing World

The world was changing in ways that she could not fathom. Soon there would be a new government. It surprised many people when they unapologetically set up a national monument where people knelt, prayed, and seemed to worship. This monument glorified what was previously considered sinful behavior. A couple of years ago this type of thing would never have been allowed. She thought of Isa. 5:20,

> "'Woe to those who call evil good and good evil,
> who put darkness for light and light for darkness,
> who put bitter for sweet and sweet for bitter'"
> (ESV).

Was this happening to society? Was up down, good bad, right wrong? If so, she thought, "Why isn't anybody challenging this? Aren't our leaders supposed to help and protect us? What happened to traditional values? How far we have fallen!" It seemed like she was the only person who cared, because she did not hear anybody else voice an opinion. "Were they scared also?" Little did she know, a trip to Europe was planned soon and would have to do with God's reason for keeping her there. She prayed for guidance and got an idea to carry tracts (gospel booklets) and bibles to hand out at the conference. "Is this idea from God and based on faith?" she wondered. She wanted to hold onto some rationale as to why God made her stay, after Danall died. God works mysteriously, as she soon discovered.

CHAPTER 3

VISION OR IMAGINATION?

Typical Day at Work

Janesth started her day in customer service, thinking about how busy one of her typical days was. In fact, there were some days when going to lunch, or even the rest room, was difficult. However, she felt thankful that she had a job and showed up for work promptly each day. After 30 years of helping customers, coworkers, and supervisors, she contemplated retirement.

Stress had taken a toll, as evidenced by several health issues. At this point, her goals were simply to do a decent job, last another five years, then drag herself out the door. Yes, those were her only goals at this point. It did not help that Janesth's normal thought process was self-condemnation and guilt, always believing she could have done better. This routinely wore her down and zapped any energy she had.

What is Happening?

One weekend she had trouble sleeping and while reclining, she cleared her mind as best she could and prayed. Something unusual happened. She thought that God was calling her, and with great excitement, she ran towards Him, seemingly at the speed of light. The closer she drew to God (who she could not describe), the more she realized that this was the best place she had ever been. Immediately she realized how sinful she was (but the thought was not allowed for some reason), and she wanted to please God. At the same time she was thinking that, she also thought, "I don't want to lose my salvation." She frequently doubted her salvation, and this weighed heavily on her. This is the place she wanted to be. "Yes!"

Lord, Am I Saved?

She had heard, "once saved, always saved," but somehow, she did not feel worthy of God's love. She could not be loved, not her, because she was so far from perfect. Did God arrange this meeting to tell her these things? She did not want to lose the possibility of being with God. What was she thinking? Seeing? Almost immediately, in her vision or imagination, God gave her a stone, put it around her neck, and impressed on her that since he put it there, she could not lose it. Overcome with joy, she stopped imagining and/or woke up. Whatever happened, she knew she had never had such an experience before. God gave her a gift in her dream, and she knew she could NOT lose it. "I cannot lose it," she said quietly.

What Will Others Think?

She was a Christian and wanted to tell others. "But wait! What would they think? Would this be considered something outside the bible (extra-biblical), and if so, this really did not happen or was a figment of my imagination. Am I losing my mind?" Janesth stopped thinking for a few minutes, then cried with overwhelming joy for what seemed like an hour. Even if she could not tell anybody, it was an experience that she believed God gave her. She wept, then slept.

When she awoke and thought about the experience, she cried again. "What happened? Was it real?" Recalling a bible story, Paul described a person going "to the third heaven," but only God knew if it was in the body or not (2 Cor. 12:2 ESV). It was like that, but still she was not sure. God had given her a stone she could not lose because He placed it there. What did the stone represent? She wanted to believe it represented her salvation, especially since she often worried about losing it. Did God give her a way to know that she is secure by His grace and mercy? She decided she would look for scripture verses to see if any supported her semi-conclusion. But where to look? In Rev. 2:17 it read,

> He who has an ear, let him hear what the Spirit says to the churches. To the one who conquers I will give some of the hidden manna, and I will give him a white stone, with a new name written on the stone that no one knows except the one who receives it. (ESV)

Janesth thought, "It talks about someone who conquers, gets hidden manna and a white stone, and a special name, but I am not a conqueror, that is for SURE! It would be awesome to get a personal name from God!" Then she remembered, "with God all things are possible" (Matt. 19:26 ESV). Doing more research, she read in Mark 9:23,

> "And Jesus said to him, 'If you can! All things are possible for one who believes'" (ESV).

Janesth reasoned, "I thought something, but do I believe? Am I saved? Is my faith real?" She persisted in her research, remembering the earlier words from Rom. 8:30, and then continued reading,

> No, in all these things we are more than conquerors through him who loved us. For I am sure that neither death nor life, nor angels nor rulers, nor things present nor things to come, nor powers, nor height nor depth, nor anything else in all creation, will be able to separate us from the love of God in Christ Jesus our Lord. (Rom. 8:37-39 ESV)

Finishing her research and confirming her belief, she read in John 20:29,

> "Jesus said to him, 'Have you believed because you have seen me? Blessed are those who have not seen and yet have believed'" (ESV).

Janesth thought through what happened. "I have seen something, perhaps in a vision, but I BELIEVE because Jesus said I should believe. Since I am saved by grace through faith, as it reads in Ephesians, I will trust God that my faith is from Him and authentic. What does the bible say faith is?" She remembered from Heb. 12:2 that Jesus is "the founder and perfecter of our faith" (ESV). Flipping back to Heb. 11: 1 she read,

"Now faith is the assurance of things hoped for,
the conviction of things not seen" (ESV).

She was finally convinced because God says we are secure in
the salvation that He alone gives us, and that salvation is based
on faith that He alone provides.

Thinking back to the vision, and still trying to come to grips
with it, she reasoned that she saw something, and somehow God
used it to show her she could not lose her salvation. Whether she
ever told anybody about this or not, would simply depend on the
future events and God's direction. She felt more at peace than
she had in a while. She continued to work hard and help others.

Sweet Retirement is Coming Soon!

Life went on for Janesth as she got closer to retirement. Her
supervisors decided to send her to a European conference where
she could share some of her vast experience with others. She started
planning for the event, and then thought, "Maybe I can take
God's word, in bibles and tracts, to share with the participants."
Because the conference included Germany, England, and Russia,
she carried those tracts. Whenever Janesth started to speak to
someone, or leave tracts, nerves set in and she decided not to. She
was hard on herself and thought, "God provided a way to share
with people in other nations, especially those who were previously
under communist rule, like Russia, and I chicken out! Why can't
I just get rid of my fear?" She knew that Christians were called
to suffer some degree of persecution, but wondered, "Should this
persecution come from myself?" Guilt and self-condemnation
overwhelmed her STILL!

Failed Again!

Feeling like a failure, Janesth headed home with a bunch of tracts. Seeing no reason to keep them with her, she stored all of them in her checked luggage and boarded the plane. Once onboard, a little woman about 90-years-old named Margie, started talking to her and eventually said to Janesth, "Oh, how I wish I had something to read in Russian." Janesth was amazed that a person would ask for Russian literature. She hurriedly looked through all her carry-on luggage, but to her dismay, could not find even one Russian tract. Apologizing to Margie, Janesth got her address, and eventually sent one to her with a sermon on cassette. While onboard for the next eight hours or so, Margie asked questions about Christianity and Jesus, and Janesth gave her a new testament bible. Janesth was amazed at how encouraged she was when somebody showed sincere interest in talking about Jesus and the bible. God opened this door. They separated in the terminal before the checked baggage arrived. Janesth was happy that God was not bound by her successes, but knew God expected His children to endure difficulties at times. He arranged the meeting with Margie, and they departed friends.

God Works in Mysterious Ways

As Janesth pondered these things, she wondered if this is one of the ways that God works with His children, by setting up meetings, and using faith to carry on the plan He set in place. As God knows when and who He will call, these things made more sense. She hoped that Margie would read the tract and call on the Lord before she died. Janesth prayed for her salvation and commended her to the Lord.

Janesth wondered, "Is there anything in the bible where God spoke to a person in a trance or vision, and called them to do something?" She read some verses from Isaiah 6. God answered her question. It records a vision Isaiah had of the Lord on a throne, with the Seraphim (having six wings), and Isaiah realized that he was sinful. They touched his lips with a burning coal, and that atoned for his sin. It turns out that God wanted to send somebody to speak to Israel, and Isaiah volunteered. Then God told him what to say. This is recorded in Isa. 6:1-10. She then thought about the Apostle Paul telling of a person going to the third heaven (not knowing whether they were in the body or not) and also seeing a vision. He was not permitted to speak about these things. Those verses in 2 Cor. 12:7-10 were,

> So to keep me from becoming too elated by the surpassing greatness of the revelations, a thorn was given me in the flesh, a messenger of Satan to harass me, to keep me from being too elated. Three times I pleaded with the Lord about this, that it should leave me. But he said to me "My grace is sufficient for you, for my power is made perfect in weakness." Therefore I will boast all the more gladly of my weaknesses, so that the power of Christ may rest upon me. For the sake of Christ, then, I am content with weaknesses, insults, hardships, persecutions, and calamities. For when I am weak, then I am strong. (ESV)

The Apostle Paul knew that God allowed him to witness certain things and experience hardships. But to Paul, these hardships seemed minor in comparison to the visions he received. It was like God provided him with the visions as motivation, to keep him going forward. He trusted God and continued in his missionary work. Regardless of its validity, her vision motivated Janesth to seek truth and work hard.

Biblical Examples

Janesth was thankful for these stories where she could look for help in her faith, struggles, and walk with the Lord. God called Isaiah and Paul, Old and New Testament heroes, to see visions. Apparently, these visions were calls from God to help establish the ministry work that they would do. The mission work was not easy, especially for Paul. As she read about his shipwrecks, beatings, being lost at sea, chased, and hated by angry mobs, she knew he paid a big worldly price (2 Cor. 11:24-27 ESV). But to Paul that was nothing compared to knowing Jesus as Lord and savior. Had they not written these passages, the bible would be incomplete. She thanked God for Paul and Isaiah's faithfulness, but knew that she was called to endure some hardships also. As she contemplated retirement, she hoped she would be faithful to her future ministry calling.

CHAPTER 4

DEAR GOD, ARE YOU STILL THERE?

Religious Beliefs?

As the day of her retirement approached, a new government was sworn in, the law-making branch was disbanded and it became part of the Executive-Judiciary (EJ). While completing exit interviews, she was surprised that they questioned her religious beliefs. "There are laws against this, at least there used to be." When asked, she gladly proclaimed herself as a "born-again Christian." That is the last thing she remembered before she woke up.

New Career and Life

Janesth did now know what happened next, and could not remember most events, except a few things from childhood, her mother, and older friends. While looking in the mirror for the first time after awakening, she saw "EI" on her forehead. She asked what it meant, but her new bosses simply said it categorized her as eligible to work in biological areas. Eventually she found out it was a new term that meant "enlightened-intolerant." Her previous pension was gone, wiped out through a new EJ order. This was like "eminent domain," except instead of property or buildings, the new national government decided it was within their rights to take money and other personal resources, including retirement packages. Since the media was controlled by the government, they did not dare reveal the extent of the corruption. Of course, when you control the laws, nothing is corrupt, or so they thought. They had free reign over the populace. Now she was starting a new career of service at age 57.

Work Hard and Serve Others

The government successfully wiped-out reminders (evidence) of her previous career, and she would not think to question them. Janesth had no recollection of God, Jesus, faith, Europe, or anything else from the past 37 years. She did not think about religion or being saved, so it did not matter, and was now a willing "biotech," who retained a strong drive for service. Remembering very little, she was not aware of any differences in her life.

Executive-Judiciary (EJ)

Shortly after the EJ was instituted as the nation's lawgiver, judge, and jury, it was discovered that many people who did not have families were easy prey for reassignment to EI status. Since she had no husband or children, and siblings and friends were no longer in touch, Janesth became an easy target. The transition to a unified global government was underway and many EIs were created without citizen suspicion. Each government dealt with the unenlightened in their own way, but if they were Christian, immediate justice or "extreme love," was deemed necessary to expedite new national plans. What was once unlawful was now encouraged. It surprised many that these changes seemed to occur overnight. In reality, they happened incrementally over the course of 100+ years. Selflessness gave way to selfishness, and public officials were no exception. They forgot their duty to the people and opted to make deals in secret. Eventually the people had no say. This resulted in the biggest national transition ever recorded. Bills did not come due on their watch, so they continued without oversight.

CHAPTER 5

Transition of a Nation

Once Great Nation

As is the case with Janesth's home country, it was a nation that had most everything they could ask for: riches, land, freedom, opportunity, justice, power, unity, food, water, natural resources, jobs, great wealth, God's hedge of protection, and generous hearts. If there was a God, and many people had their doubts, He certainly blessed this nation. Although there were many people who would agree that they were blessed, some thought they were treated unfairly and challenged the status quo, thus blaming "whoever they could" for their predicaments. The louder they cried, the more the nation gave into their demands. No matter how obvious it was that their behavior was self-destructive, the media, courts, government, schools, and society decided they were right and everybody else was responsible. Blame continued despite efforts to right past wrongs. In fact, they eventually got their civil status changed to a protected class, based on emotions, lifestyle choices, and other factors.

Over half of the people, 90% of the courts and schools, and 95% of the media agreed that these groups were abused in some way. The cry from those still able to speak (typically Christians) resounded with, "work hard, get educated, provide selfless service, and trust God." As time went on, these sayings were considered the nonsensical ravings of religious fanatics and eventually outlawed. Was perception reality, or was there an objective truth?

The Destruction of a Nation

As things changed, exponential regression occurred. People said, "How can this be? What happened to our nation that was so blessed?" Despite some efforts to steer the nation back to sanity, unemployment (population not working) rose to 50% and welfare to 60%. Drugs, alcohol, sex, credit, material possessions, and denial now offered no solace. Hope was gone for many. Due to anarchy and other things, the EJ initiated their secret agenda. Rabid EJ sycophancy was able to execute the plans, with little suspicion, limited oversight, free rein, and no mercy! Unless it served the EJ's purposes.

As plans progressed, the media served their new master well. Investigative reporting happened only to EJ opposition. Private citizens battled government, media, and endless litigation, which became an exercise in futility. Funding eventually ended, as did their freedom. This led to radical tyranny. However, to show their fairness and objectivity, the EJ made examples of some caught committing crimes. Many of these criminals previously worked under the EJ's supervision, but they lost favor by either getting caught or outliving their usefulness. When terminations occurred, people said, "Satan is firing his minions." Of those terminated, half authored books favorable to the EJ, and the others wrote scathing reviews. People blamed each other but talk shows always presented favorable opinions. The press shielded the EJ against negative attacks, so newfound "consciences" never saw the light of TV. The EJ was a mean master, and those who worked for them knew it.

Transition to the Future

Eventually, many of the nation's laws were simply overturned, or re-written, by unelected judges, so unhappy people (other than religious) learned that they simply needed to cry "unfair" or "unjust" and the law would eventually change or go away. Since the law-making branch was now an arm of the judiciary, remaining nonbelievers were routinely convicted of speaking against the new protected classes. Many of the incarcerated were let out with vindication certificates that read they were grossly misjudged. They were now entitled to carte blanche (as restitution for their false sentences) which amounted to remuneration worth twice the length of their time served. The nation was bankrupt.

Prisons Cost Too Much

Since the state did not want to risk paying these penalties, new law-breakers were not imprisoned but simply given items to wear on their clothes to show that they were bigoted, unyielding intolerants unwilling to accept the new normal of society. After two breaches of the new laws, these folks were branded with a mark that showed their noncompliance. This led to an inability to buy, trade, or live. They cried daily to God, "Please help us!" There seemed to be no help for these unprotected, who kept weeping, wailing, and dying.

Unenlightened Intolerants

Throughout all this, there remained the "unenlightened" who kept proclaiming faith, repentance, and something about a Jewish savior named Jesus (their reason for living as Christians). This was the first group where torture was formally approved, but it was often called "extreme love." As extreme love became the norm, not only were more of these unenlightened lying in the streets bleeding, but the enlightened started believing they had another good reason to work. Beating intolerants became a vital activity for many. When the new EJ branch realized that beating intolerants caused less crime in other areas, they mandated the practice. Eventually, many intolerants died off, converted to enlightened status (by adding a branded "E" (like animals) to their forehead), or went into hiding. Jobs for the newly enlightened depended on a few things. Since they had previous marks from brands and tattoos, they became servants or porters, then assigned the menial duties of cleaning contaminated dumps. The number of dumps increased because every environmental practice was permitted. After several cleanings, enlightened-intolerants (EIs) were assessed for bodily change. With EI on their forehead, this group was easy to recognize. Moreover, using integrated circuit chips meant they could be tracked easily, and any physical or mental changes could be recorded in the EJ databases.

Societal Change and Its Effects

After a few years, with the seeming end of intolerants, societal norms continued to evolve, and the medical profession became more proficient in identifying new ailments. These ailments were often easily blamed on intolerants. As the EJ called for the creation of new prevention methods, disease cures were discontinued. Since doctor and nurse professions were eradicated, and research funding was now used for security, bio-med-technicians became the nation's certified medical professionals. Strict and detailed checklists were used and enforced, with levels of prognosis given to every person for each event. Levels 1 through 4 meant the government would provide some additional care, and levels 5 and 6 meant that a person could choose to terminate. Since painkillers were outlawed at levels 5 and 6, and there was some talk of eliminating painkillers completely, it became easier for people to request termination. This helped with the EJ's mandated goal of negative population growth. Since it was now established science that humankind destroyed the planet, it was only right that humans eventually eliminate themselves. The irony of societal change was that many who were the most vocal and violent against Christians, were at one time persecuted themselves. They did not care what happened to this group, because the only thing it was NOT okay to be, was a Christian.

Population Decreases but Problems Increase

Due to increased solar activity, inability to get people to farm (or farms to produce), continued wars especially in the Middle East, thousands of daily terrorism deaths, and drastically reduced natural resources, worldwide population decreased. With births being outlawed by mandatory contraceptives, it was no surprise that the earth's population went from eight to four billion in three years and five months. Yet for some reason, there was not enough food, clothing, or medicine for the enlightened citizenry. In the past it was easier to blame intolerants, but many were now eliminated or in hiding. Those found were beaten mercilessly. This never lasted too long since beating intolerants did not produce food, and even this eventually got old.

CHAPTER 6

BURIED TREASURE!

Contraband

One day during a routine cleaning of an old bio-medical facility, Janesth found a book. It was written in English and Spanish and on the cover, it read, "Holy Bible/Biblia." Janesth realized that she would get into big trouble looking at contraband (designation for Christian and Jewish books), with an immediate Level 6 designation, and wondered what she should do. Her curiosity peaked, and since this might be the only chance to look at such a book, she decided to skim through it. This book was unusual from any she could remember but thought she had seen one as a little girl when her mother Esther taught that God was loving and kind. She remembered that faith and grace were important. On page 1, where it was sectioned off as Genesis 1:1 it read:

> "In the beginning, God created the heavens and the earth" (ESV).

She wondered, "If there really is a God, did He create this?" Skipping ahead to a section called Ps. 14:1 she read:

> "The fool says in his heart, 'There is no God.' They are corrupt, they do abominable deeds, there is none who does good" (ESV).

"The EJ would NOT want to see this! They say they are the greatest good and demand service and obedience. Anybody who wants to live MUST agree with them." Janesth spoke quietly, "This book basically says that the EJ is foolish." Skipping ahead to Matt. 2:11 she read about a baby born in a manger, and wise men who brought gifts,

> "And going into the house they saw the child with Mary his mother, and they fell down and worshiped him. Then, opening their treasures, they offered him gifts, gold and frankincense and myrrh" (ESV).

"Worshipped a baby!?" The EJ outlawed babies except for rich people and/or experimentation. Searching the bible, she learned that someone named Herod wanted to kill Jesus, but his parents took him to Egypt for protection (Matt. 2). She thought, "If anybody could understand the current plight of babies, it would be Jesus. Why do powerful people want to kill babies?" She cried because of the many ways that babies were treated, and then terminated, in society. "How can this be?"

Who is this Baby in the Bible? Jesus?

She was perplexed and getting more afraid, but reluctantly skipped ahead to learn more about the baby that these wise men worshipped. In John 14:6 she read:

"Jesus said to him, 'I am the way, and the truth, and the life. No one comes to the Father except through me'" (ESV)

"Jesus says he is the way and truth and life, and talks about the father. What is this? The way?" She dared not "dog-ear" the page even though it seemed important, because that might be used as evidence against her. Continuing, she came to 1 John 1:9 and read:

"If we confess our sins, he is faithful and just to forgive us our sins and to cleanse us from all unrighteousness" (ESV).

"Forgive our sins? What sins?" As soon as she thought those words, she knew she was a sinner, and more importantly, needed forgiveness. "This book is the truth, and truth does not change" (M. Pitts, Sermon, May 15, 2016). She wondered, "How many things approved by the EJ would be considered sin? Is Jesus really alive?" She kept going back and forth then read:

"For all have sinned and fall short of the glory of God, ..." (Rom. 3:23 ESV).

"Yes God, I know I am a sinner. PLEASE forgive me. Help me, please." She momentarily forgot where she was. She remembered from childhood that faith and grace were important. But why? "God, if you are real, if you are there, please help me to know about grace and faith."

Saved by Grace through Faith

She flipped again through some pages and read:

> "For by grace you have been saved through faith.
> And this is not your own doing; it is the gift of
> God, not a result of works, so that no one may
> boast" (Eph. 2:8, 9 ESV).

"Wow! Thank You God! Faith IS important. I want to be saved, God, Jesus, please give me faith." If Janesth could just remember that she placed her faith in Jesus as a young girl. Nevertheless, she (again) started to place her faith in Jesus and believed that God was real.

Called?

She thumbed ahead to Jude 1:1-2 and read:

> "Jude, a servant of Jesus Christ and brother of
> James, To those who are called, beloved in God
> the Father and kept for Jesus Christ: May mercy,
> peace, and love be multiplied to you" (ESV).

"Called?" She thumbed back and forth and saw many places where the word "called" was used. "How does God call a person?" She chuckled, "Maybe he lets us find bibles in garbage dumps and reads to us." Suddenly she was not laughing. Was God calling her? If Janesth could just remember her previous life, husband Danall, trip to Europe, Margie, the countless times that God called and blessed her in seemingly trivial things, and then always provided the help she needed. Little did she know that God was working in and through her circumstances where she needed him.

God Remains Faithful

He remained faithful and seemed to adjust his methods based on her needs. She thought, "Yes, he is calling me." In a silent cry, she knew this was a most loving moment from God, and placed her faith in Jesus (again), who she admitted she did not really understand yet. She began to learn more about Jesus, that he came from heaven, lived a perfect life, died on the cross, rose again, and intercedes for us in heaven. She needed him as her savior. Time was short. What did she need to do?

Revelation of Christ

Janesth knew that if she did not report back soon, she would be questioned. Almost finished she thought, "But what does this chapter called 'Revelation' mean?" It reveals information about Jesus, the Christ. In Rev. 1:1-3 she read:

> The revelation of Jesus Christ, which God gave him to show to his servants the things that must soon take place. He made it known by sending his angel to his servant John, who bore witness to the word of God and to the testimony of Jesus Christ, even to all that he saw. Blessed is the one who reads aloud the words of this prophecy, and blessed are those who hear, and who keep what is written in it, for the time is near (ESV)

Angels, John, Prophecy?

Janesth knew she was in trouble because she was late, but wanted to read the prophecy aloud so she could be blessed. Her situation was starting to seem hopeless. Alarmed, she read in Rev. 13:16-18:

> Also it causes all, both small and great, both rich and poor, both free and slave, to be marked on the right hand or the forehead, so that no one can buy or sell unless he has the mark, that is, the name of the beast or the number of its name. This calls for wisdom: let the one who has understanding calculate the number of the beast, for it is the number of a man, and his number is 666. (ESV)

"Whoa, wait a minute! Beast? Number? That is happening today." For some reason she thought of a popular product. "Was the logo really formed by connecting three consecutive Hebrew sixes?" It did not matter since many people would not care, even if they knew. But whether they cared or not, she still thought it was important to say something about Jesus and salvation. "Shouldn't this be obvious to everybody? How can we not see the things that are happening? We have marks on our bodies, and if we did not, we could not live or eat." Janesth thought of the hunger she would have from not eating, and often passed by many such people in the streets.

Dread came over her, but for the first time (that she recalled), she realized God IS love and has persistently called people for years. Overwhelmed by what she learned, she thought, "Will Jesus really save me?" She remained fearful, even though they altered her memory. God pursued her however, and in Rom. 10:9 she read:

"Because, if you confess with your mouth that Jesus is Lord and believe in your heart that God raised him from the dead, you will be saved" (ESV).

Janesth opened her mouth and said aloud, "God help me! Yes, Jesus IS Lord, and yes, you raised him from the dead." She held one finger on the verse, and let her other finger move forward and read:

"For 'everyone who calls on the name of the Lord will be saved'" (Rom. 10:13 ESV).

Saved from What?

Flipping through the pages Janesth read:

Then I saw a great white throne and him who was seated on it. From his presence earth and sky fled away, and no place was found for them. And I saw the dead, great and small, standing before the throne, and books were opened. Then another book was opened, which is the book of life. And the dead were judged by what was written in the books according to what they had done. And the sea gave up the dead who were in it, Death and Hades gave up the dead who were in them, and they were judged, each one of them, according to what they had done. Then Death and Hades were thrown into the lake of fire. This is the second death, the lake of fire. And if anyone's name was not found written in the book of life, he was thrown into the lake of fire. (Rev. 20:11-15 ESV)

At this point she was frightened, but she KNEW she had confessed with her mouth what it said in Rom. 10:9. She believed God, but still thought, "Lake of fire! No, no, please no Father God, Jesus Lord...help me...save me, save others...forgive me, forgive us...please...I did not know!" She knew she was safe. "But what about others who have not heard this message?" She was sad for them.

Grace or Justice?

God answered her questions from the bible; He was indeed a God of grace and justice. She thought, "How terrible it would be for those who would experience His justice, because that means God would judge them, and if no one is righteous, then some will pay a terrible price. People need His grace and mercy! If only people knew that they could simply ask God?" She was happy that God was patient, but knew that would not last forever. "People MUST call on the name of the Lord." She flipped to the end of the bible and read,

> "He who testifies to these things says, 'Surely I am coming soon.' Amen. Come, Lord Jesus! The grace of the Lord Jesus be with all. Amen" (Rev. 22:20-21 ESV).

CHAPTER 7

LOVE'S LAST CALL

Mystery and Fullness

Yes, come Lord Jesus! She thumbed backed in her book and read,

> "Lest you be wise in your own conceits, I want
> you to understand this mystery, brothers: a partial
> hardening has come upon Israel, until the fullness
> of the Gentiles has come in" (Rom. 11:25 ESV).

"Fullness, mystery, hardening, come in...huh? God, does this mean that there is a point when you will stop calling?" At that moment she wondered if God knew when the last person he called would be saved. She thought to herself, "Of course, he knows everything, right? Could it be me, the next person, the person after that?" If it is truly God who calls, she could not help but wonder why more people were not saved. "How many hidden bibles would be found today, tomorrow, the next day, in dumps, closets, shelters, or garages?" She felt a sense of urgency. "Please guide, help, strengthen, and encourage me, Lord!"

Called Despite Persecution

Jesus said,

> "'Remember the word that I said to you: "A servant is not greater than his master." If they persecuted me, they will also persecute you'" (John 15:20 ESV).

"Yes," she thought, "Persecution is coming my way!" She was thankful that God spoke to people, but obviously in diverse ways than she was used to. It was apparent why the EJ had penalties for those reading the book because it went against everything they taught. Angrily, she thought, "Lies, lies…the world loves lies! Even though levels 5 and 6 were death penalties, what harm would it do to let them hear God's word?" She then realized, "Doubting God's word, that is the oldest temptation in the bible" (M. Pitts, Sermon, May 15, 2016). Suddenly she could sense the pure evil involved with preventing people from giving "terminals" (those condemned to death) hope before they die. "That hope IS Jesus, and terminals must hear this message. People must share! Many people just accept that Levels 5 and 6 terminal designations were enemies of the EJ and condemned to die lonely, fearful, and painful deaths. Oh God, what should I do?"

Why Doesn't Society Love You God?

Janesth supposed that there could be comfort for these people, if only they knew that God loved them. "Why God are you not loved or wanted in our society?" That question haunted Janesth as she pondered her inevitable re-designation. She decided to keep the book hidden from the EJ but would try to share it with others. If the EJ found it, they would certainly change the wording, or make an example of the one found carrying it. That warning in Revelation was real! She wondered how many of the words in this book would be changed, disregarded, or removed by the EJ to mean something else. If they got the book, it would be discarded or shelved until a time it could be used for other (propaganda) purposes. "How many problems would be eliminated if we call to God using His words?" As she contemplated things in her society, she was saddened that many would never know about her Lord Jesus Christ.

The hour with the book changed her, enlightened her, and God saved her. How could a hopeless existence be changed so quickly? As she wept over her newfound savior and friend, she could only look down thinking of things, she wished she had done differently. She prayed,

> "Jesus, please forgive me, help me, and embolden me to share your word with others. May they also confess you as their Lord."

God Continues His Call in Europe

In Europe, Margie was in failing health, and asked her family to open the package she received from the young lady on the plane. Although she did not speak English perfectly, she was able to understand the sermon on the tape recording. Her great-granddaughter read the Russian tract to her, which presented Jesus as the way to eternal life. As her body lay close to death, she asked God to save her, and accepted Jesus as her personal savior. She died on earth, but continued life in heaven! "Thank You Jesus for saving me," Margie said as she entered paradise.

CHAPTER 8

FAITHFUL AND TRUE!

Hallelujah!

As she was changed, Janesth committed at that moment to tell others, no matter the cost. She bowed in prayer, then her head started looking skyward, and heard something amazing,

> "'Hallelujah! Salvation and glory and power belong to our God, for His judgments are true and just;...'" (Rev.19:1b-2a ESV).

Words continued, then she saw something; a white horse!? Could it be Him!? She looked forward in Rev. 19:11 and read,

> "Then I saw heaven opened, and behold, a white horse! The one sitting on it is called Faithful and True, and in righteousness he judges and makes war" (ESV).

Reality Meets Prophecy

She realized that the Bible was open, and she was reading it as prophecy was fulfilled. Stunned, overwhelmed, and filled with unspeakable joy, she knew that God had allowed her to see this. Janesth's redemption drew near. He was coming! Rejoicing she thought, "All this time, God was the answer, not the blame. He has been calling people for about 2,000 years." Trumpets sounded and the air smelled clean. Things changed because her memory was restored, lost all her fear, markings were gone, and instantaneously knew the reason she was kept back when Danall died.

The last thing Janesth thought was, "'Do not disbelieve, but believe,'" (John 20:27b ESV) like God was finally taking that from her mind. How many times did she doubt and re-believe, only to relearn of God's faithfulness?

Speechless, then Paradise

She was speechless! What happened next was too wonderful for words, but immediately many things made sense. Margie, standing with Danall, welcomed Janesth into paradise. God remained faithful, no matter how many times Janesth doubted. She felt blessed that she found the bible when she did.

Numerous Little Things Remembered

As she continued her new life in heaven, Janesth saw many other redeemed people. It was exciting to learn that they spoke of their unlikely encounters with Christians who prayed for them and many others. Everybody had a similar story, being drawn by God's love. Their prayers made it to the Lord's ears. Some listened and shared stories, and others even gave their lives. Many gave tracts, bibles, rides, DVDs, tapes, notes, stories, resources, time, money, meals, help, encouragement, bible studies, watched pets, did yard work, painted homes, provided security, and showed hospitality. Still others visited prisoners, the sick, injured, elderly, and lonely, while others oversaw mission trips and administrative functions. Doctors, nurses, medical professionals, and dentists quietly helped people in need, often without others knowing they were Christians. In churches many pastors and staff members prepared and led worship teams, sang songs, played instruments, delivered the gospel and reports, gave sermons, watched children and elderly, babysat, and delivered flowers and meals. Many shared personal testimonies and did other works that seemed too numerous to count. These little things were part of a larger set that God's "called" did. And finally, as written in James 1:27, some went,

> "To visit orphans and widows in their affliction"
> (ESV).

Once called, and saved by grace through faith, her brothers and sisters did good works, not to earn their salvation, but to demonstrate their love for God through faith. Their saving faith resulted in good works, some large and some small, some many and some few, but all important AND for the glory of God and the good of His children. It would not surprise Janesth if all the redeemed loudly and excitedly said together,

> "For we are His workmanship, created in Christ
> Jesus for good works, which God prepared
> beforehand, that we should walk in them"
> (Ephesians 2:10 ESV).

Faith seemed simple, but it was not always easy. Living now by sight, she remembered what she had previously read,

"So faith comes from hearing, and hearing through the word of Christ" (Rom. 10:17 ESV).

Little Things as Part of God's Bigger Plan

Yes, God worked through the unimportant things so people could hear the word of Christ. One day, Margie thanked Janesth for the airplane conversation, gospel presentation, prayer, tract, New Testament, and sermon tape, which helped her realize she needed Jesus as her savior. Because of God's faithfulness and His willingness to use weak, foolish, and despised people, and materials like tracts and tapes, Janesth realized that she was used in God's bigger plan.

While on earth, Janesth recalled that her prayer, especially when she started praying for a new person was, "Dear Lord, please open their eyes, ears, mind, and heart, so they can see, hear, believe, and be saved." Looking around in her new home, and seeing many happy redeemed people proclaiming similar words, she could not yet understand fully how God answered all her prayers, but one thing was certain, "He did! Yes!" She loudly proclaimed that, "God was, is, and will continue to be, AWESOME! Forever and EVER!"

Margie was His last call. Janesth and Margie had eternity to become great friends, to worship and love God, and to hear countless stories of His faithfulness. God proved to be Faithful and True. Danall's murderers were there also. They were saved after their convicted friend told them about Jesus. If more people had accepted God's gracious gift, their eternity would be with Him, instead of an eternal separation apart from Him. Jesus spoke often of this other place, and it is called hell.

The end.

CHAPTER 9

CONCLUSION AND LESSON

I hope you enjoyed the story, it resonates meaningfully, then leads you to Jesus. Margie was eternally grateful that God had her meet Janesth. If we ask God to open eyes and hearts, people can see and believe. Then we can help them walk in doors that He opens later.

Why Did I Write This Book?

God had mercy on me and I want others to receive His gift. Jesus told stories, people listened, and then shared throughout history. In our story, tragedy struck a nation because it put idols (false gods) before the true God. These included pantheism, lying, cheating, stealing, toleration, evil schemes, political correctness, immorality, selfishness, greed, heartlessness, etc. This violated God's commandment,

> "You shall have no other gods before me" (Exodus 20: 3 ESV).

This is biblical. In Isa. 46:1, God spoke about Babylon's idols and "weary beasts" who bore these "burdens" (ESV). Isaiah. 47: 9 shows the two things" that strike fast; "the loss of children and widowhood" (ESV). Janesth lost her husband, had no children, and became easy prey for evildoers. In truth, citizens will suffer, just like Babylon did, under nationalized idolatry. An idolatrous nation should expect to hear,

> "You felt secure in your wickedness, you said, 'No one sees me,' your wisdom and your knowledge led you astray, and you said in your heart, 'I am and there is no one besides me'" (Isa. 47:10 ESV).

If we forsake God and trust idols, catastrophe follows. In Numbers 10:2, Moses had "two silver trumpets" made for use in "summoning the congregation and for breaking camp" (ESV). Numbers 10:8-9 reads,

> And the sons of Aaron, the priests, shall blow the trumpets. The trumpets shall be to you for a perpetual statute throughout your generations. And when you go to war in your land against the adversary who oppresses you, then you shall sound an alarm with trumpets, that you may be remembered before the Lord your God, and you shall be saved from your enemies. (ESV)

Final Thoughts

Is God warning us? If so, let us confess, repent, and be contrite. When leaders place idols, we ALL bear the burden. This is like the death humankind suffered when Adam and Eve sinned. Hear the trumpet?

NEW WOLF

DEDICATION

To God the Father, Son (Jesus), Holy Spirit, Jan, Loving Family, and Friends.

ABOUT THE BOOK

These are 2nd edition works of fiction. Most of the main ideas for both stories came before the latest world events, personal experiences/worldview, and imagination. If you like it, share with others. If there are errors, I apologize, and will make corrections by hand in printed books (if possible) and soft copies before further printings. Your understanding is appreciated. This is a ministry that I hope you will participate in by sharing this book, and more importantly, your own testimony and The Bible, with others. Jesus shared stories; let's do the same and encourage others!

PRAYER FOR READERS

Father, Dear Lord God, Your word reads, "And this is the testimony, that [You] God has given us eternal life, and this life is in His [Your] Son. Whoever has the Son has life; whoever does not have the Son of God does not have life" (1 Jn 5:11-12). Please open eyes, ears, hearts, and minds so we can see, hear, believe, and be saved. Help us to love You with all our heart, soul, mind, and strength and love our neighbors as ourselves. Give us saving faith, restore hope, teach us to be loving, kind, compassionate, encouraging, generous, and truthful, to work hard, be thankful and fearless, seek wisdom, and trust You! All praise, glory, and thanks to You! In Jesus' Name I pray. Amen. Love, Dan

CONTENTS

CHAPTER 1

PROLOGUE

Garden of Eden

In our enlightened world, believing in the Garden of Eden, Adam and Eve, and Jesus rising from the dead may seem like fairy tales to many people. Many others believe it to be true. If these words from the Bible are true, then God created humankind in His own image with certain basic rules. We were to trust and obey Him. Our first parents did not trust and obey, so we (all humankind afterward) inherited the penalty for that original sin. Let that sink in for a moment before we proceed.

If we were to imagine some scenes in slow motion (like a movie projector) through history we might see some things both good and bad. If humankind had not sinned, all these scenes would be good because our behavior would have been in obedience to God. Instead on our movie projector we may see (or recall), death, plague, holocaust, terrorism, Christians beheaded by antichrist zealots, death, anger, rage, hostility, starvation, murder, abortions, rapes, and hating God and our neighbors. Screens are unique to each person. Other scenes might include Israel becoming a nation again and getting Jerusalem back, Martin Luther King, Mother Theresa, and countless good works by millions of people around the world. Since many will never read the Bible, I will suggest some verses to look at to help us grasp the significance of sin. Then we can decide if we would like to act to do something for ourselves.

As a Christian I must try to point out that Jesus is our only hope, even if others say He is not. He paid a dear price as you will see in this chapter. The story that starts in chapter two shows how mankind's continuous sin resulted in a gross misrepresentation of God's designed order. Sin has consequences. There could be millions of stories like this one. Thank God those stories have been reduced because of Jesus. Adam and Eve were in paradise and God gave them some essential guidance that required trust and obedience. According to the Bible the sequence went like this:

> "The Lord God took the man and put him in
> the garden of Eden to work it and keep it. And
> the Lord God commanded the man, saying, 'You
> may surely eat of every tree of the garden, but of
> the tree of the knowledge of good and evil you
> shall not eat, for in the day that you eat of it you
> shall surely die.'" (Gn 2:15-17).

God gave His command and man understood. Evil then spoke and lied about God. Humankind, although fully able to trust and obey at that point, decided to disobey God. Sin entered paradise and our world:

> "Now the serpent was more crafty than any other
> beast of the field that the Lord God had made. He
> said to the woman, 'Did God actually say, "You
> shall not eat of any tree in the garden?" And the
> woman said to the serpent, We may eat of the

fruit of the trees in the garden, but God said, "You shall not eat of the fruit of the tree that is in the midst of the garden, neither shall you touch it, lest you die." But the serpent said to the woman, 'You will not surely die. For God knows that when you eat of it your eyes will be opened, and you will be like God, knowing good and evil.' So when the woman saw that the tree was good for food, and that it was a delight to the eyes, and that the tree was to be desired to make one wise, she took of its fruit and ate, and she also gave some to her husband who was with her, and he ate" (Gn 3:1-6).

Separation and Death (consequence #1)

God spoke, humankind disobeyed, then consequences followed. These included consequences for all involved: the serpent, Eve, and Adam. Please take a few minutes to read Genesis 3:13-19 to see the extent of God's righteous anger. Some may say at this point, "Come on, what is so bad about that? We do much worse and it does not seem like God is upset." It might seem that way, but if humankind indeed died at that point, what does that mean? Are we alive as God intended? Smarter people than me will have to address that question. If death meant dying physically and spiritually, then I (think) that is what it means. For now let us assume that humankind suffered both kinds of death. Adam and Eve eventually died physically and so will the rest of us. We just do not know how long we must live in our physical bodies.

What about spiritual death? In our modern world we pursue many avenues to spiritual enlightenment. Are they correct? From my personal experience most of these paths start with the word "self" and are a restatement of the same old lie the serpent told in the Garden of Eden. The serpent said, "For God knows that when you eat of it your eyes will be opened, and you will be like God, knowing good and evil." Pick any "self" or "false" religion / philosophy and see how God's Word is changed to make you the master of your domain, knowing right (good) and wrong (evil), eyes now opened, and empowered to achieve your dreams. How much money, sweat, and tears are lost before a person realizes they were duped?

Jesus said we must be born again. If we must be born again, that means we must be dead spiritually and brought to life. The key here is that God is the one who gives the new life. People may wonder what Christians mean when they said they are "born again." We simply know the supernatural power of God brought us to life, by faith. The Bible reads:

> "Jesus answered him [Nicodemus], 'Truly, truly, I say to you, unless one is born again, he cannot see the kingdom of God'" (Jn 3:3).

Garden of Gethsemane (consequence #2)

In Genesis 3:15 we see part of the effect of the fall on the serpent and the seed of the woman (Jesus). Although it might not seem perfectly clear in this verse, God is explaining what must now happen. Her offspring (Jesus) will be wounded because of this original sin. This is no minor wound, it cost Jesus His life as He paid for our sins. This prepared the way for us to have the spiritual rebirth required to be with God again; eventually in heaven. Our new birth includes His Holy Spirit. If that is not great news, I do not know what is!

> "I will put enmity between you and the woman,
> and between your offspring and her offspring; he

shall bruise your head, and you shall bruise his heel" (Gn 3:15).

This bruising of the woman's seed allowed our reconciliation with God the Father. And payment was only possible through Jesus' sinless sacrifice on the cross. He fulfilled the law, prophets, and psalms (Lk 24:44). What a terrible price He paid, but He was the only one Who could do it. God provided the sinless lamb that we needed because we could never pay our sin debt. Please read the Biblical account of that part of Jesus' ordeal in the Garden of Gethsemane in Matthew 26:36-46.

Golgotha (consequence #3)

The bruising of the woman's seed continued until Jesus said, "It is finished and He bowed His head and gave up His Spirit" (Jn 19:30b). From Gethsemane to Golgotha our Lord sweat blood, was brutally beaten, publicly humiliated, slandered, spit on, mocked, then forced to carry the instrument of His death. Then He suffered the most agonizing and painful death for us. Earlier I posed the possibility that some might say. "What is the big deal? That was not so bad." Yes, it was and still is, for those who do not trust in Christ. If we are born again by God's Holy Spirit, we are becoming more like Jesus. If not, the logical conclusion is that we will continue the path toward complete spiritual death; whatever that might look like. Three days after He died on the cross Jesus rose from the dead. In other words He conquered death. The question:

"Who did Jesus conquer death for?"

If there really is a hell, and Jesus spoke about it frequently in the New Testament, then that place is reserved for some. What is it about our current physical life that makes it so hard to look at the eternity of life? The Bible tells us that there is a heaven to be gained and a hell to be avoided. Is there a way to avoid the place called hell? Yes.

Eternal Death or Life (consequence #4)

> "I told you that you would die in your sins, for unless you believe that I am he you will die in your sins" (Jn 8:24).

> "Because if you confess with your mouth Jesus is LORD and believe in your heart that God raised Him from the dead, you will be saved. For with the heart one believes and is justified, and with the mouth one confesses and is saved" (Rom 10:9-10).

The Story That Follows

Sin has consequences. As we look from the Garden of Eden to Gethsemane to Golgotha to today, we see that God has been faithful, but is profoundly serious about His word and law. He said trust and obey but humankind disobeyed. That original sin remains in all of us. The following story is a fictional account of what might happen in a world that hates God. I hope that you are edified and inspired, but heed the warnings, in the following story. May God bless you and His church as He makes disciples and saves the lost. Thank you.

CHAPTER 2

NEW WOLF EXPELS CHRIST

Scene opens at the world court as Christianity is found guilty and outlawed. It is no surprise. Lawlessness has become the way of the world:

> "There is no such thing or person as God! Now
> we can have peace," many proclaim.

Laws are no longer used openly. Evolution is true, so power to the fittest. The last official act of law enforcement is to get the remaining lawmakers to safety in pre-established remote locations like islands, mountains, and deserts. Mass hysteria has taken over the streets around the world. Five-page pamphlets are being dropped everywhere. Sex, crime, drugs, and alcohol are available to everybody who desires them and now takes place openly. Anyone who gets offended is beaten or killed.

Newspaper Office

In a local newspaper where John Ramon, reporter for the Southwest Interrogator, gets an assignment to cover changes resulting from the court's decision. He is not too surprised and has been a self-proclaimed agnostic since his first year in journalism college. "Christianity is not based on objective truth, but more on fairy tales and myth."

The final world court rulings read:

1. Marriage and childbirth are outlawed.
2. Honor only New WOLF, not mother and father.
3. Death is the greatest good.
4. Quoting the bible is outlawed and punishable by immediate execution wherever it occurs.
5. Murder is legal except for certain "un-kill-ables."
6. National sovereignty and borders are outlawed.
7. Survival of (and for) the fittest. Kindness is unlawful unless to gain some advantage.
8. Objective truth and personal responsibility are outlawed. Feelings and opinions are paramount.
9. In all other cases where guidance is absent, "Law is unlawful." All courts are abolished except as permitted by the New WOLF.

After reading the information that came over the newspaper wire John Ramon said:

> "It is about time! This world can finally come to our senses."

An elderly assistant named Rose slips and falls in John's area and asks for help. He replies:

> "Haven't you heard old woman it is against the law to show kindness."

He throws a pamphlet to her and says:

> "When you get yourself up, maybe you want to look at this. Do not tell anybody I gave it to you!"

Almost immediately John thought about his mother:

> "Once she dies I can be a true citizen of the world because any reminder of caring will be gone. What a wonderful world we now live in!"

The pamphlet really was quite simple and based on evolution and the strongest surviving. It had five pages, most of which gave examples of the new world changes. John Ramon had just given a practical demonstration of what life would be like now for the weaker and older citizens. The only thoughts allowed were those that were hateful, unhappy, chaotic, impatient, unkind, not good, unfaithful, harsh, and lacked self-control.

On page 4 of the pamphlet readers saw how people could establish new behaviors based on whatever is false, ignoble, incorrect, impure, ugly, detestable, mediocre, and condemnable. Being a journalist, John had the new pamphlets immediately after the law was made. Rose writhed in pain and cried, but she received no help. What was about to happen to the world was a combination of evil and grace fighting each other. New WOLF represented established evil and the bands or packs of Christians displayed God's mercy and grace. John reflected on the irony of the world losing objective truth:

"New WOLF outlawed objective truth. The essence of world legal changes was based on legalism, subjectivity, and opinions of a few. If people had a chance to look at the facts, no such decision would ever be allowed. How would this affect objectivity required in journalism?"

CHAPTER 3

HER READINGS ARE HIGH

A computer operator picks up a Red Flag on his monitor. Rose Smith is identified as a potential threat because her emotional and cognitive readings (ECRs) exceeded acceptable ranges. She has clearly exceeded the established 50% threshold authorized for each citizen. As the day went on, there are many other readings at the 80-90% level. These elevated readings were later found to indicate people in pain or suffering, and especially those who were praying for themselves and others.

After the law was changed and 100% of the citizenry monitoring occurred, it could be more accurately determined who had higher ECRs; implants were given to every citizen. It was exceedingly small and inserted through inoculations. Eventually the implant, which was designed to attach in the brain as a clot, would cause death. Developers did not care because death was now the ultimate good. Either the implant provided ECRs, or stopped emitting a signal which meant the person was dead. Elevated readings could also indicate that people had peace, as brought on by prayer. Generalized anxiety should be the norm, because the last thing the New WOLF wanted was happy citizens. After three errant ECRs, people were marked for termination.

Fred Hernandez, a Baptist pastor in the middle of Arizona watched the news without blinking an eye. He whispered to himself:

"This day was bound to come. Oh God!"

The last church service consisted of 23 people (down from last year's average attendance of 284), and the offering was just enough to pay for drinks and snacks. As the people filed out of the church, Pastor Hernandez sees that Rose is visibly shaken and tries to comfort her with a hug and kind words. She is taken aback by the gesture since such behavior is not allowed in the pamphlet.

CHAPTER 4

NEW WOLF'S PAMPHLET

"With the merciful you show yourself merciful;
with the blameless man you show yourself
blameless; with the purified you show yourself
pure; and with the crooked you make yourself
seem tortuous" (Ps 18:25-26).

As Pastor Hernandez thought about Rose and the state of the New
World (WO) Legal (L) Force (F)(WOLF), he wondered how
they produced the pamphlet. Anybody who worked anywhere had
to read the pamphlet 10 times before starting their workday. This
was turning into an effective way to indoctrinate people. Where
did the idea for the pamphlet come from? Wait! He suddenly
realized that this was the exact opposite of Galatians 5:22-23 as
he recalled from memory:

"But the fruit of the Spirit is love, joy, peace,
patience, kindness, goodness, faithfulness,
gentleness, [and] self-control."

The following verse read:

"Against such things there is no law" (Gal 5:23b).

"Yes, being kind was now against the law," he thought. It seemed extremely hopeless for him, the church, and those searching for meaning. He prayed:

"Dear Lord, please have mercy and help us, especially Rose and the elderly."

They were the weakest and most vulnerable, and Pastor Hernandez knew that their days were numbered. He thought:

"The world is backward."

Until the pamphlets started dropping out of the sky it was common to hear many people say:

"Woe to those who call evil good and good evil" (Is 5:20).

"Yes," he thought, "The woes have been multiplied!"

Monitoring Station

In the desert of middle Arizona, a man named Brent Davis and his friend Todd Wilkins stopped to rest and take shade in a cave. As Brent walked around, he heard a barely audible click. Thinking he must have stepped on a branch he never thought twice about it. On the other side of the cave wall was a maintenance & operations room with people that monitored every move the men made. Around the globe there was a similar station every 1000 square miles. They were completely self-sufficient and when the time came, would have access to enormous amounts of food and ammunition. These cave dwellers would eventually resurface to reinsert themselves into society after the initial purge of citizens. The total population must be depleted by two-thirds (2/3) to make the New WOLF unstoppable. By instituting unrestrained lawlessness, they were assured of instantaneous deadly results, especially for those who did not consider themselves Christians. Even for those who did, they realized that some Christians would participate in the carnage. Hungry and angry people can do abominable things. Many people had been spared from death by the likes of Brent and Todd, who stopped many merciless killings. The New WOLF leadership never intended for Christians to remain alive after the first 100 days (about 3 and a half months), but they were thriving and helping each other.

"That simply will not do," said Colonel Bert Jones.

Colonel Jones was the commander responsible for getting the world's death toll to 50% in 45 days. After leaving the cave, another click occurred which went unnoticed by Brent and Todd.

CHAPTER 5

WHAT DOES MAGPIE DO?

In this you rejoice, though now for a little while, if
necessary, you have been grieved by various trials,
so that the tested genuineness of your faith—more
precious than gold that perishes though it is tested
by fire—may be found to result in praise and
glory and honor at the revelation of Jesus Christ.
Though you have not seen him, you love him.
Though you do not now see him, you believe in
him and rejoice with joy that is inexpressible and
filled with glory, obtaining the outcome of your
faith, the salvation of your souls." (1 Pt 1:6-9).

President & General

In 2005 when the idea of MAGPIE was first brought up, it was
a way to cease fire using command & control. A few years later
the thought of controlling private weapons became too good to
be true. Many of the highest-ranking officials did not know about

this but the general officers and homeland security did. One question that started to rise in General Ford's (GF) mind was:

"If we had control of these weapons, why didn't we stop school and airport shootings?"

There was no doubt in her mind that these weapons were equipped with MAGPIE, since they were made after 2009. Dare she ask her Commander in Chief? She had decided that she must.

GF: "Madame President (P), with all due respect, who has knowledge of MAGPIE besides the Defense departments and Pentagon?"

P: "General Ford you have broached an extremely sensitive subject and I will not answer your question. It is need to know and I deem that you do NOT need to know!"

GF: "Madam President again with all due respect, being the ranking armed forces member I not only have a legitimate need to know, but must ensure the technology is used lawfully, and not by our enemies foreign and domestic. We just cannot pass up the opportunity to use MAGPIE to save lives if possible. The recent school shootings and airport terrorism could have been avoided had we used MAGPIE in a defensive way. Many innocent people lost their lives."

P: "That will be all General Ford. You have not only crossed a line but have certainly shown your lack of respect and cooperation given the times in which we live. MAGPIE is no longer just a national asset, but now belongs to the world community. You are dismissed!"

GF: "But Madam President what about…?"

P: "I said you are dismissed!"

The general left the President's office but wondered why such an asset was being shared with many who were no doubt their enemies. After General Ford had left, John Marshall entered the president's office through an obscure, almost hidden door. Looking at President Margaret Williamson he said:

"That could be an issue!"

She smiled, nodded, and knew what she had to do. On her way-out General Ford knew she had better not say even one negative word regarding the situation she had become aware of. She knew she was on her own, but as a General Officer who took an oath to protect and defend the constitution, she believed there was the potential for misuse of this defensive weapon known as MAGPIE. She decided to notify her Congressional representative, Senator, and the FBI to see if an investigation was warranted.

She could not recall a time when she felt so low. Being the first woman to become the highest-ranking military member was something she was proud of, but calling for a pre-investigation of another government source, and the first woman president, was something she took no joy or satisfaction in. Were any people killed because we decided not to use MAGPIE? If so, where did the blame lie? She prayed:

"Dear God, if you are real, please help me!"

Little did she know at the time that God was working in a very mysterious way.

MAGPIE (Magazine Pull/Interfere/Extricate)

In the mid-2000s, researchers started to experiment with gun safety devices. These could provide some safety for children had they mistakenly, or intentionally come across their parents' guns in the home. Researchers looked for ways to disarm children and criminals who held loaded weapons. After 100s of trials and errors, a system was developed called MAGPIE that used various mechanisms to disable guns (depending on the style). Some of these disablements resulted in anywhere from a few seconds to an hour or more of malfunction. Since this was extremely sensitive and seemed to be a violation of the 2nd Amendment, it was thought to have been discarded. In 2008 with the stock market crash and worries about guns getting into the wrong hands, some unethical research practices took place.

In gun manufacturers, government and contract-testing overseers were asked to ensure that final safety precautions and operational tests were completed, and MAGPIE installed. During the stamp and serial number verification and validation confirmation, a small, yet effective, super-strong infrared and magnetic device was put into all handguns and rifles under the serial number and riveted into place. Once the MAGPIE device, which would be used at necessary times, was activated, it would take magazines and clips that were inserted into the weapon and adjust them just enough to cause a malfunction. Most weapons operators would simply remove the clip or magazine, clear the weapon, and try again. The goal of the application was to stop the weapon from firing just long enough (until help arrived). When the new administration in 2009 heard of this technology and application, they added a more prolonged capability of non-fire, right under the noses of the gun makers. This was significant since government involvement with gun makers as a test agency lacked objectivity and impartiality at that point. Yet they oversaw the installation of MAGPIE, something that the government should have stopped.

The irony is that objective testers became subjective and destructive to many gun owners who simply wanted to be personally responsible for themselves and families. The President at the time was John Marshall who served for eight years and perfected MAGPIE. Now he served as the Vice President (VP) under the current, and first woman President, Margaret Williamson. Many people at the time raised concerns because a person could not serve as President more than eight years. This was challenged in the Supreme Court (SC), and it was decided that many VPs served under Presidents before becoming President, why not have it the other way around. This of course would only be a problem if something happened to the President. The next person in line would legally be the Speaker of the House. Since this person was considered semi-conservative, many people did not see the harm in such a departure from the norm for Vice Presidents. John Marshall held onto his current identity but did not rule out subjective interpretations of law that allowed people to self-identify. He kept that information close to his chest like a well-seasoned poker player. He put into place many justices who agreed with his perception of legalese and everything was to be open to subjective interpretation.

MAGPIE was successfully tested in a few situations, but on occasion was unsuccessful in stopping weapons fire. Even so, the probability of success was high. The million-dollar question was:

> "Why didn't they actually use the technology to
> stop known massacres and terrorist events?"

That was a question that many people would want answered if MAGPIE ever became known by the public. Gun manufacturers and owners did not know what had been put in place. Had they known, many people would have marched defiantly on the nation's capital. For now, they were happy with their right to bear arms. What good would a dysfunctional firearm do if people or their families were ever attacked or endangered?

CHAPTER 6

WHO TO TRUST?

General Ford was despondent and sought the counsel of another 4-star general officer in her same service branch. Assuring each other that this would be held in strictest confidence, General Ford explained what she believed happened in the two most recent massacres. The friend and comrade was stunned. Yes, she should pursue a meeting with the Armed Services committee. While talking about their days at the academy, they both realized how much their careers had meant to them, and what a great pleasure it was to serve their country. It surprised General Ford when her friend asked if he could pray with her and she agreed. He closed the prayer in Jesus' Name and General Ford said:

"Boy, I sure could use Jesus' help right now!"

Her friend Bill replied:

"Then let's make sure you are right with Him."

He presented the gospel, and she accepted Jesus as her savior, although she seemed to remember doing that as a little girl. She felt relieved but knew she was responsible for making sure that ALL enemies, foreign and domestic, were held accountable. She just could not help but think:

> "Why do people think and act the way they do? Why is it okay for some people to behave in certain ways and not others?"

Finally, she thought:

> "There is something dreadfully wrong when judges make completely different decisions after looking at the exact same information."

After 38 years of being a soldier, she knew leaders had to process information and make decisions, but to knowingly do something illegal or unjust is wrong. She wondered:

> "This subjective, capricious, and arbitrary reasoning is just plain wrong. Everybody must be treated equally, otherwise the scales of justice are unbalanced!"

NEW WOLF Devours Leadership

She thanked her friend, they walked out of the building together, and while respectfully saluting each other, a black van reigned bullets at both generals, killing them instantly. Her story would not be told. In fact, technically, a crime had not been committed unless they were on the list of un-kill-ables. They were not, because their names were mysteriously removed from a database minutes before. That is how they knew to eradicate them. Both generals' next conscious moments occurred in heaven. They looked around and thought:

> "Why is there such a big army and what are they getting ready for?"

NEW WOLF Devours Innocents

Rose was at her wits end and could hardly function because of stress brought on by her boss John Ramon (JR). She knew that John's mother laid near death and often prayed for her, silently of course. This might be one of the many elevated ECRs she elicited on the computer monitoring system. John, having been informed that Rose was marked for termination, could only think of his mother and how New WOLF would certainly come for her also, if she were not so close to death. As John approached Rose (R), he showed no mercy and let her have it with all the hatred he could muster, as prescribed by the New WOLF pamphlet. Rose started to cry, then felt an overwhelming sense of compassion for John. It was like she could see his pain and fear. In fact, looking at John she saw a scared little boy. John stopped, and then the strangest thing he could remember happened; he cried and asked for Rose's forgiveness.

R: "I forgive you John, but there is somebody else you may want to speak to."

JR: "Who?," he asked.

R: "Jesus."

JR: "I can't call on him, I am too guilty and besides, they will Kill me too if I do."

R: "John, from what you have told me your mother has prayed for you since you were little. God works in mysterious ways, and this world will not get better for you or for me. Jesus is the sinner's friend. If you know you are a sinner, please ask him to help you."

JR: "Yes, yes, yes, I know I am a sinner. Jesus, please help me, Rose, my mother, and even this world. Please save me Jesus!"

Another salvation miracle had occurred in an office in the middle of Arizona. As John walked Rose down to the termination station, he was informed that he too would be terminated. He was very scared, then looking at Rose, wondered what would happen to his mother but he knew they were related in Christ and shared a boundless joy that could not be understood. The next conscious moments they had were in heaven, but instead of standing with Rose, he was standing with his mother. Her prayers were answered. God had mercy on him, and he knew he did not deserve it. He thought:

> "What is going on here? White horses? What are they getting ready to do?"

NEW WOLF Devours Patriots

Brent and Todd arrived at another remote location for a break and a recon. Some reports had shown that the former world leaders hid in many of these areas. They were not looking to fight and wanted to avoid firefights if possible. They had families that were killed by people bent on death and destruction. Their goal was to help people know Jesus, but to stay alive if possible. While walking around the area, Brent heard a click like the one earlier.

He started to dismiss it again, but suddenly the cave opened and out came ten heavily armed men with orders to:

"Drop weapons!"

Caught off guard, Brent and Todd sought cover and waited for fire. They were told that their weapons were useless and no longer worked. In disbelief, Brent tried to fire a shot into the air. Nothing happened. Todd did the same thing. Nothing. They removed and reinserted the rifle magazines; still nothing. After checking their pistol clips, they knew further resistance was useless. Three of the men came over to them and (apologetically) told them about MAGPIE. Brent and Todd were discouraged and wondered how long they mistakenly believed they had a fighting chance, when they had none. Suddenly Brent and Todd looked at each other and wondered how many Christian soldiers were walking around helping the less fortunate, only to be sitting ducks for anybody with knowledge of MAGPIE. Seeing that they had just walked into a death trap, they tried to run. They were hit in the back almost immediately. Laying there, one of the New WOLF soldiers (S) came over to put them out of their misery when Brent (B) said to him:

B: "I am getting ready to go home. Praise my Lord Jesus!"

S: "You mean you are getting ready for a long dirt nap."

B: "Yes, certainly my body will be settling in the dirt, but my soul and spirit will be with my Lord Jesus in heaven."

S: "Jesus? The world court just outlawed him."

B: "Yes, but He is King of kings and Lord of lords and is coming back some day" (Rv 19:16).

At that time Todd prayed silently for the soldier and his family, then passed away. Brent asked:

"Can you remember a time when somebody spoke to you about Jesus?"

S: "Yes, my grandmother when I was a little boy."

B: "Isn't it nice to know that she would be there to meet you in heaven when you die, if you trust in Jesus?"

S: "Yes, but if I do, they will kill me too."

B: "This is a scary time, but please accept my prayer."

Brent prayed for the soldier and as they both said "Amen," Brent breathed for the last time on earth. The soldier knew Brent was right and asked Jesus to save him. The squad leader (SL) came over to the soldier and said:

SL: "What did they have to say? Something about Jesus, I suppose."

S: "Yes, something about Jesus."

Brent and Todd were consciously alive in heaven. Looking around in their new surroundings, they thought:

"Heaven is awesome, but what are all these horses and people doing here?"

As the soldier returned to the cave, he noticed on a monitor that many Christians were being mercilessly beaten in various places around the world. He prayed, asked for forgiveness, and felt so sorry for these innocent victims. In an unusual moment, the soldier started to pray for the salvation of his team leader and squad. He knew they needed hope also. God just worked a miracle in him so he hoped He would also save his friends and family.

NEW WOLF Devours Law

Similar incidents occurred throughout the eight years of the current president. The year before President Williamson left office, John Marshall, current VP, and previous President, announced his intention to run for President again. The masses decried such an outrageous violation of the constitution. However, due to a recent Supreme Court (SC) decision, self-identification was the law of the land based on gender, race, color, or national origin. Technically, according to the SC, a person could have multiple identities and receive benefits for each. Social security numbers and other benefits were now available for each identity if it was registered with the government. The more identities a person had, the more enlightened they were understood to be. Christians were considered the most unenlightened because they considered themselves one with Jesus Christ.

John Marshall (male) could not be President, but Joanne Marshall (female) could be. He had not undergone transgender surgery, but because he really felt truly transformed, was now considered a "new creation" according to New WOLF and the national government, which gave up its sovereignty after most political enemies died or were killed. In an egregious and blasphemous act against the Holy Bible and Holy God, soon-to-be President-elect Joanne Marshall said:

> "Therefore, if anyone is in the New WOLF, their identities are new creations. The old identities remain but behold new identities have been added for value to the person and world communities. Those with the most identities are worthy of praise and worship. For the transgender, transracial, trans-color, and transnational are indeed most enlightened. The more identities each citizen has, the more opportunities to become one with the

universe. Constantly proclaim and admire these new identities on TV, radio, and Internet. They are the loveliest beings" [grotesquely modified from 2 Cor 5:17].

Of course, this was another evil attempt to alter the true Biblical Word of God which correctly read:

"Therefore, if anyone is in Christ, he is a new creation. The old has passed away; behold, the new has come" (2 Cor 5:17).

As Pastor Hernandez watched in sadness and disillusionment, he realized just how much the current world had changed as many churches adopted new beliefs, words, and practices that were contrary to the Bible. Knowing in his heart and through countless empirical evidences and individual experiences that the Holy Bible was the true inerrant and infallible Word of God, he knew he must stay true to its teachings, whether it cost him his life or not. The statement by Joanne Marshall was further evidence of mankind's unwillingness to accept Jesus as the true Lord of His creation. He cried for what seemed like an hour, then went to sleep. If only this was a bad dream. He thought:

"Oh Lord, we have certainly reaped what we sowed" (Gal 6:7).

Although self-identification was abhorrently subjective, five SC justices determined that a single identity could be President for eight years. If a person changed their identity, she could serve eight more years. Technically, even if he did not have the surgery, a person could simply claim a different identity, and that new identity was allowed to be President of the United States. The number of identities a person could have was limitless. This went against God's law, objective truth, and common sense. The New WOLF hated God, and especially Jesus, and they knew multiple identities served their agendas and eliminated unwanted laws.

NEW WOLF Devours Friends

Up until now "friends," consisting mostly of liberals, progressives, and wanna-be elites were exempt from the harassment that was dealt to law-abiding Christians or so-called "right-wing fanatics." Now, these friends of the former government were considered outcasts because NEW WOLF no longer saw value in using them to achieve their goals. These former friends, now known as "outcasts," had served their purpose to achieve the desired end (establishment of New WOLF) and they were useful "means." These outcasts were discarded like used up trash. Since all goals were achieved, the government started treating them worse than Christians because these outcasts knew secrets, processes, and the whereabouts of various subjective tentacles that were used to justify laws, rules, decisions, and unfair practices. Although it was unlikely that any outcasts could cause trouble, NEW WOLF's unlimited power made it quite easy to deal harshly and quickly to stifle any dissent. Many screamed:

> "What happened to our special treatment and favor from government?"

> "How could we be treated this way after all we have done? Please God, make them give us what we deserve. We have been cheated!"

Christians Embrace Outcasts

Many outcasts eventually became Christians, shared their testimonies, and were subsequently hated even more by New

WOLF. However, some Christians could hardly restrain their negative comments because they were still being changed, but not yet perfected through God's sanctification process. It was typical to hear Christians say:

> "We tried to tell you, but you would not listen. It
> is your own fault."

As God convicted Christians, they knew that it was only grace that saved them and the outcasts. Forgiveness happened frequently. As reality set in, outcasts committed suicide at extraordinarily high rates. Some were even heard yelling:

> "Oh God, why did you let this happen?"

Some did attach themselves to Christian church groups because without government support, they were helpless. Christian groups were the only people that would help them. They cried:

> "How could we be so blind?"

Churches were the only places where there was still hope when things seemed to be both good or bad. People started asking the important question:

> "Who is Jesus?"

THE LORD Jesus was pleased to open many eyes, ears, hearts, and minds to believe the gospel. Many wondered why it took so much pain before they believed. They were incredibly sad that they treated their new brothers and sisters so badly in the past. It surprised them that they were forgiven because their new family members did many of the same things before their conversion to Christianity. It was all starting to make sense. Outcasts simply had nowhere to go. Slowly, they realized they were duped and were of no use to their former friends. As subservient minions who knew too much, their first thought was to hide themselves. But where? Who would help? As they found themselves in the streets begging, selling themselves, and asking for money, liquor, drugs, and anything else that would ease their pain, many Christians came to their side and presented the gospel of Jesus Christ. Outcasts were usually unwilling to listen because of New WOLF's indoctrination that Jesus was a myth. This did not stop Christians from presenting the gospel because many genuinely believed that God's Word was the power to save. In fact, they often said to the outcasts:

> "For I am not ashamed of the gospel for it is the power of God for salvation to everyone who believes, to the Jew first and also to the Greek" (Rom 1:16).

Many outcasts were reluctant, but others thought about their own mortality and life after death:

> "Could these Christians be right about hell? Could this religious stuff be real? Is Jesus who they say he is?

Christians kept presenting the gospel (or as they called it, the power of salvation). They would often cite Romans 10:9-10:

> "Because, if you confess with your mouth that Jesus is LORD and believe in your heart that God raised Him from the dead, you will be saved. For with the heart, one believes and is justified, and with the mouth one confesses and is saved."

Outcasts often responded with:

"Saved from what?"

Many Christians said:

> "You will be saved from eternal separation apart
> from God and extreme agony and suffering. What
> we are dealing with now is no comparison to what
> hell will be like."

That often got the outcasts' attention, but God started working
in their hearts, so they asked to see some verses about hell in the
Bible. They were surprised to see that there were many times
that Jesus spoke about hell. One of the last things they usually
said was:

> "But I am so sinful, guilty, and dirty; God would
> never love me."

Christians often replied that the outcasts would be surprised
at what they had done before being saved. The key was God's
mercy and grace, not their works or own righteousness. When a
person is saved, Christ's righteousness was imputed to them.

After sharing with each other the sins they had each
committed, outcasts and Christians agreed that if left to themselves
they deserved punishment. Christians maintained that Christ's
righteousness was the only thing that would save them, and faith
in Him was needed. One of the last things that was typically told
to the outcasts was:

> "Or do you not know that the unrighteous will not
> inherit the kingdom of God? Do not be deceived:
> neither the sexually immoral, nor idolators, nor
> adulterers, nor men who practice homosexuality,
> nor thieves, nor the greedy, not drunkards, nor

revilers, nor swindlers will inherit the kingdom of God. And such were some of you. But you were washed, you were sanctified, you were justified in the name of the LORD Jesus Christ and by the Spirit of God" (1 Cor. 6:9-11).

Many recent outcasts (O) thought that they were serving God by doing anything and everything they could for their former and newest government. They eventually found out that their beliefs and actions were opposite of those in the Bible. As they spoke with those they formerly persecuted, they started to realize that Christians (C) were simply trying to trust and obey their LORD Jesus. As they began to learn more, and God started convicting their hearts, conversations between Christians and outcasts usually sounded something like this, especially after they were presented several scripture verses. These scripture verses pointed to Jesus who came from heaven, died on the cross, rose from the dead, ascended into heaven, and one day would return to get His bride (the church).

O: "But I am not righteous, and God would never love me! What have I done? Help me God. I have hurt and had killed many of these loving Christians."

C: "If you know you have sinned, that means God is convicting you and showing you the truth. He has begun to open your eyes, ears, heart, and mind so you can see, hear, believe, and be saved. If Jesus is calling you, please answer Him. He is truly our only hope. In 1 John 1:9 the Bible reads, 'If you confess your sins, He is faithful and just to forgive your sins, and purify you from all unrighteousness.' After listening to you, I know that God has shown these sins to you. Other especially important verses were Romans 10:9-10 (shown above). Do you know you are a sinner? Would you like to be forgiven and spend eternity with Jesus and have eternal joy?"

O: "Yes, Jesus please save me and my family. I know I have sinned and cannot fix myself. Have mercy on me LORD Jesus."

C: "Thank God that He has called you into His family. These sufferings are temporary, but God has given His Son, the LORD Jesus to pay our sin debt. Are you ready to pray with me? Let us pray to the LORD Jesus. He is our only hope and only way to be saved."

O: "Thank you and thank God. I needed Jesus' righteousness and He is giving it to me by faith."

Faith in Jesus was a new concept for many. They called on Jesus and rejoiced because the truth was revealed to them. Many thought almost immediately after praying the "sinners' prayer" (like the one in Appendix B. God wants our heart, not our works of righteousness). How ironic that many spent their lives putting NEW WOLF into place but now knew their hope was only in Jesus, who they had persecuted their entire lives. Many people were saved from hell.

CHAPTER 7

CONCLUSION

The SC decision and subsequent re-election of a person with a second identity was the last straw for patriots. They stormed every vestige of government throughout the land. Unfortunately, as they drew close, they had no idea what was about to hit them. The New WOLF massively applied the MAGPIE application effectively disabling 98% of the weapons for at least five minutes. The casualties of those who fought against New WOLF was 99.7%. Some people were kept alive for training and intelligence purposes. Patriot families were exterminated with extreme prejudice. Many gave death site gospel testimonies to their killers. It is unknown how many of those killers accepted Jesus at that moment, but knowing the power of God the Father, the Son, and His Holy Spirit, Christians had confidence in God's persistent call.

As Pastor Hernandez and many church leaders around the world prayed, although their faith was being tested, they knew they could trust in their LORD Jesus Christ. As many hoped this might be near the end, they looked to the book of Revelation for encouragement. In Revelation 19:11-16 they read:

"Then I saw heaven opened, and behold, a white horse! The one sitting on it is called Faithful and True, and in righteousness he judges and makes war. His eyes are like a flame of fire, and on his head are many diadems, and he has a name written that no one knows but himself. He is clothed in a robe dipped in blood, and the name by which he is called is The Word of God. And the armies of heaven, arrayed in fine linen, white and pure, were following him on white horses. From his mouth comes a sharp sword with which to strike down the nations, and he will rule them with a rod of iron. He will tread the winepress of the fury of the wrath of God the Almighty. On his robe and on his thigh, he has a name written, King of kings and Lord of lords."

Pastor Hernandez and the small church continued to live by faith. His eight church members knew Jesus is returning soon! In today's Bible study they read:

"For I consider that the sufferings of this present time are not worth comparing with the glory that is to be revealed in us. For the creations waits with eager longing for the revealing of the sons of God. For the creation was subjected to futility, not willingly, but because of him who subjected it, in hope that the creation itself will be set free from its bondage to corruption and obtain freedom of the glory of the children of God. For we know that the whole creation has been groaning together in the pains of childbirth until now. And not only the creation, but we ourselves, who have the first-fruits of the Spirit, groan inwardly as we wait eagerly for adoption as sons, the redemption of our bodies" (Rom 8:18-23).

Pastor Hernandez sighed and prayed silently:

"Come quickly Lord Jesus. Nevertheless, not my will, but yours, be done" (Lk 22:42).

He *hoped* Jesus might be getting ready to say something like:

"It's time! The call is complete. My creation has groaned long enough and My bride awaits!"

If so, countless prayers would be answered and Jesus woud return soon. Oh, the glorious joy for His bride!

"Amen. Come, Lord Jesus!" (Rv 22:20b).

The end.

CHAPTER 8

EPILOGUE

Is the Holy Bible the inerrant and infallible Word of God? I believe that it is. A person may ask, "How did you come to that conclusion?" For me personally I heard the gospel, believed, then went out and sinned like the worst heathen on the face of the earth. Why? I loved my sin and was not discipled. That is one reason discipleship is so important. When God saves you, He does not leave you where He found you. Thank the Lord for that! In this story a couple of the soldiers recalled hearing the gospel as children. God was faithful and remembered that call, even if they did not due to extreme circumstances. God allowed the soldiers to hear His good news again, from soon to be perishing saints.

Before we are saved, we are condemned to an eternity apart from God. Once we are saved by grace through faith, God starts His sanctification process in us. In other words, He is changing us. I highly recommend that you read Romans 1; the entire chapter. In verse 16 we see that the gospel is the "power of God for salvation." That is awesome! Keep reading. Starting in verse 18 we read about the "wrath of God" being revealed from heaven. Continue reading verse 32. If God does not save us, we will have one or more of the unrighteous characteristics including "envy, murder, strife, deceit, maliciousness, gossip, slander, haters of God, insolent, haughty, boastful, inventors of evil, disobedient to parents, foolish, faithless, heartless, [and] ruthless" (Rom 1: 29a-31). Many of us still struggle with one or more of these, but God is faithful; He transforms us as we repent.

Objectivity is based on facts and subjectivity on feelings and opinions. If we were to look at the varying opinions of laws and how they are frequently reinterpreted, we should get an idea of how subjectivity impacts our courts, commissions, decisions, and way of life. Should it be this way? One person may say that feelings are facts. Yes, but only for that person or maybe a few others. Are these feelings trustworthy to make decisions? No.

In this story we saw what can happen when subjectivity reigns. If somebody genuinely believes they should be classified as a different gender, should that feeling be the basis for comprehensive legal changes for everyone? And this does not just apply to gender. If people in authority decide to impose their strongly held subjective beliefs for law, marriage, religion, life, death, etc., how will this impact our world? This is happening in our society today. Do research and decide for yourself.

APPENDIX A

GOOD NEWS, FUTURE REALITY, & STRATEGY

We are saved by God's grace and mercy. If God is calling you, please answer Him. Let us see what God's word says:

> "And this is the testimony, that God has given us eternal life, and this life is in His Son. Whoever has the Son has life; whoever does not have the Son of God does not have life" (1 Jn 5:11-12).

> ""And it shall come to pass that everyone who calls on the name of the Lord shall be saved""" (Acts 2:21).

Jesus is God's one and only begotten Son. After Adam and Eve sinned by disobeying God's command not to eat from the "tree of the knowledge of good and evil" in the garden of Eden, we inherited the death sentence that God warned them about (Gn 2:17). As a result, it is part of mankind's nature from that point on. This sin caused everyone's spiritual death and separation from God. Therefore, our spirit needs to be brought to life by God's direct intervention when we are saved or "born again." God is both merciful and just. We may think our good works will outweigh the bad. Even with millions of good works, we are not good enough, because God requires perfection (Jas 2:10).

> "'You therefore must be perfect, as your heavenly Father is perfect'" (Mt 5:48).

Jesus died for our sins, and we receive his PERFECT righteousness by faith, as God's loving gift. Jesus is the "founder and perfecter of our faith" (Heb 12:2).

What Happened?

God's Son (Jesus) came to earth, lived perfectly, fulfilled the law, and died on the cross. God raised Him up. He is now in heaven and is LORD. Do you believe that? If so, you have saving faith. If not, pray and ask God for saving faith.

> "'There is no other Name under heaven given among men by which we must be saved'" (Acts 4:12).

If you know you are a sinner, confess your sins to God and repent:

> "If we confess our sins, he is faithful and just to forgive us our sins and to cleanse us from all unrighteousness" (1 Jn 1:9).

Appendix B has a prayer for salvation. Be honest with God and yourself. His Holy Spirit provides the power to repent and change.

Future Reality: Heaven or Hell

Jesus is the most trustworthy person who ever lived and spoke about heaven. Heaven is paradise and boundless joy.

1. "'Pray then like this: Our Father in heaven, hallowed be Your name, Your kingdom come, Your will be done, on earth as it is in heaven'" (Mt 6:9-10).
2. "And Jesus came and said to them, 'All authority in heaven and on earth has been given to me'" (Mt 28:18).

Jesus also spoke about hell. It is a place to avoid because it is filled with extreme agony, pain, and suffering. There are many other verses about hell. Remember, tomorrow is not guaranteed.

1. "'And do not fear those who kill the body but cannot kill the soul. Rather fear him who can destroy both soul and body in hell'" (Mt 10:28).
2. "'You serpents, you brood of vipers, how are you to escape being sentenced to hell?'" (Mt 23:33).

Strategy for the Way Ahead

See the prayer in Appendix B. If you have accepted Jesus as Lord, that is awesome! You are now part of God's family. To grow in that relationship, you might want to follow these suggestions:

1. Pray and ask God to help you grow and learn. Read the bible a chapter a day, starting with the book of John. John 1:1 is a profound subject to think about.
2. Pray and ask God to help you find a Bible-believing, preaching, and teaching church. They will support you.

3. Pray and spend time with God every day. It is best if it is quiet. If you have a spouse, you might want to plan a daily or weekly joint prayer and/or study time.

4. Give, "for God loves a cheerful giver" (2 Cor 9:7). As you mature as a Christian you want to give more.

5. Find out who needs prayer. Pray for them and yourself.

6. We will still have times when we sin so let us confess to God, and ask Him to help us repent and trust Him.

7. Get a study/accountability partner to share (pray for) each others' struggles. BE HONEST. Seek God's help.

> "Therefore, confess your sins to another and pray for one another, that you may be healed. The prayer of a righteous person has great power as it is working" (Jas 5:16).

8. We may be tempted to think we have things under control and point out others' sins. Beware of this!

All Christians are sinners saved by grace. We should love God with all our heart, soul, mind, and strength and love our neighbor(s) as ourselves. Set your thinking on the things in Philippians 4:8 (true, noble, right, pure, lovely, admirable, excellent, & praiseworthy). Do and practice the things in Galatians 5:22-23 (love, joy, peace, patience, kindness, goodness, gentleness, faithfulness, & self-control). In today's world we may strive to be independent and rely only on ourselves. As Christians, we begin moving from our own agenda to God's agenda. We should try to "trust and obey God in all we do."

> "Trust in THE LORD with all your heart and do not lean on your own understanding. In all your ways acknowledge Him, and He will make straight your paths" (Prv 3:5-6).

"'The LORD bless you and keep you;
The LORD make His face to shine upon
you and be gracious to you;
The LORD lift up His countenance upon you and give you peace'"
(Numbers 6:24-26).
Amen.

Love, Dan

APPENDIX B

PRAYER FOR SALVATION

Father, Dear Lord God,

Thank You for being there to hear my prayer. You know me, I am a sinner and I have my doubts, but I want to be saved from an eternity apart from You. Please give me saving faith, help me to repent, and forgive my unbelief. I know I need Jesus as my Savior and I want to trust Him as my Lord. I trust Your Word and confess right now, with my mouth, that "Jesus is Lord." I "believe in my heart that God [You] raised Him from the dead" (Rom 10:9). Please put me on the path You are calling me to and help me repent of my sins. Thank You Jesus for dying on the cross for my sins and redeeming me. I love You, praise You, and give You all the glory. In Jesus' Name I pray. Amen.

Love,

YOUR NAME, _____

TODAY'S DATE, _____

ABOUT THE AUTHOR

Dr. Danny Hurd has a Doctor of Business Administration (D.B.A.) in Management Information Systems, a Master of Science in Information Systems Engineering, and a Master of Counseling. He is married to Janice, has two sons (Rob and Mike), two daughters-in-law (Sherryl and Cindy), and three granddaughters (Dani, Zoey, and Zara). Danny served in the US Army (retired Chief Warrant Officer) and Department of Defense (both as a Civil Servant and contractor) for about 35 years. He is currently an Adult Education and Literacy instructor at Wharton County Junior College. As an Operational and Interoperability Test Director, he stressed the importance of objectivity, facts, and fairness for systems' evaluations in typical operational environments. He believes faith in Jesus Christ is paramount, the Holy Bible is the inerrant and infallible Word of God, and "The Ligonier Statement on Christology" accurately reflects Biblical Christianity. The statement can be found at http:// christologystatement.com/.

BOOKS BY THE SAME AUTHOR

OUTLAWED! Objective Truth & Personal
Responsibility (Nonfiction)

Printed in the United States
by Baker & Taylor Publisher Services